When The Wicked Play

A Dark Romance Novella

Tristina Brockway

Cover by RJ Creatives

Edited by Briggs Consulting LLC

Formatted by Unalive Promotions

Trigger Warning

This book contains scenes that may depict, mention, or discuss assault, attempted murder, attempted rape, blood, child abuse, death, gun violence, hospitalization, murder, physical abuse, rape, sexual abuse, sexual assault, torture, violence, and more.

Dedication

For those with a story.
I believe you.

Playlist

Wicked Ones - Dorothy
Spiders - RAINNE
Demon Mode - Stileto, AViVA
Dark Side - Bishop Briggs
Darling - Halsey
Kill Of The Night - Gin Wigmore
Wicked Game - Lusaint
Nightmare - AViVA
Mood Swings - billie
Villian - MISSIO
Mother's Daughter - Miley Cyrus

Playlist available on Spotify.

Contents

Prologue

Charlie

The slow drip of a leaky faucet would have driven most people mad from the constant noise. It's as if a never-ending echo from a pipe throbs against my eardrums, but I find the incessant dripping soothes my mind. It's often the only sound I hear for days at a time.

A continuous, putrid odor fills my nose with each breath I take. The humid, frigid air that clings to my skin should leave me chilled from the inside out, but it seems to be a part of me now. The growing numbness to my body is engulfing any ounce of warmth I may have left in not just my body, but my soul.

I'm uncertain how long I've been here. Time appeared to stand still when I first arrived, but eventually one second turned to ten. Ten seconds turned to ten days and now it very well may have been ten years.

I was young when I was first dumped here. My name seems like a distant memory, but I've somehow clung to it. As if the name alone can give me the identity that was stripped from me.

I can't remember many details, but I remember the

feeling of dread and heartbreak. For myself or someone else, I'm not exactly sure anymore.

The men come down to pay me a visit in my personal hell more often than I'd like, but sometimes it's desperately needed, assuming I want to have food and water. Sometimes wanting to stay alive is more of an inconvenience than anything else, but my behavior lately says quite the opposite.

They don't like it when I fight back. After all this time, I still have the will to live, which doesn't do me any favors. I assume they wouldn't keep me chained and half-starved if they had any interest in killing me. Then again, any food and water are better than none and that alone might prove me wrong. After all, why would you feed a corpse?

Chapter One

Charlie

I struggle to take a breath and begin to choke and cough on the substance that fills my throat and lungs. I'm surrounded by something, but I can't see and can barely move. I try to lift my arm, but I'm met with a barrier. Wiggling my fingers, the sensation in my hands returns.

The particles I'm slowly inhaling with each breath I attempt to take feels like coffee grounds but smell like dirt.

Why do I smell dirt? I don't just smell it. I'm suffocating on the odor and I'm thinking it's not just the odor that's depriving me of oxygen, but the substance itself. I move my hands as fast as I can, reaching for what I can only hope would be air on the other side.

Every sensation in my body hums. I'm hyper aware of this moment. A fight to survive if I ever had one. The sudden feeling of spiders and insects creeping along my skin in their own struggle to survive me mauling at the dirt surrounding us has me digging even faster.

I see light as I finally break through the earth and struggle to pull my face towards the fresh air so that I can finally get the unobstructed breath I've been seeking for what feels like an eternity, but in reality, has probably only been minutes.

Whoever tried to kill me did a piss-poor job. You know, considering I'm still breathing. *Barely.*

I crawl along the ground away from the shallow grave they dumped me in and try to take in my surroundings while continuing to cough up the dirt that slid past my lips while struggling to breathe.

It must be night or early morning. The temperature feels cool and crisp. I can see my breath, but not so much that it's freezing. As I look down, I realize they have left me for dead in a shallow grave, completely naked.

"What the fuck?" I murmur to myself as I look down and take in my state of undress, only to cough up more pieces of dirt from my scratchy, dry throat.

I wrap my arms around myself for any bit of warmth I can find and squint my eyes to try to figure out where I am. Even though the sun is not out my eyes are sensitive from being closed and blanketed in darkness while under the earth. I can only guess that's from the drugs they flooded my system with to presumably end my life.

Looking around, it appears I'm in the middle of nowhere. It's still dark out and I'm struggling to see clearly, but I can hear the faintest sound of what I think may be an occasional vehicle passing by.

I hear a small chuckle slip past my lips, which then turns into a giggle. And eventually the giggle leaves me outright belly laughing, gasping for breath.

I've lost it. *I've fucking lost it. Haven't I?*

Struggling to catch my breath, I touch my face and pull my hand away to find my fingertips wet from the foreign liquid I forgot was streaming down my face from my leaking eyes. *Are those tears?* Surely I'm not crying. I can't remember the last time I let tears fall and now it's been so long I'm not even aware of it.

Wrapping my arms around my stomach again, I walk toward where I heard a faint sound of traffic, stumbling over branches and wading through the freshly fallen leaves that weren't lucky enough to evade the fall climate or the death it left in its wake. The tree line isn't visible enough to see what is waiting for me up ahead.

My feet feel frozen and numb and I'm trembling from the cool night air brushing against my naked body as I walk through the thinning woods.

I would hate not having a way to tell the time. I could never have a watch or clock and any time I asked what time it was, they punished me in some form or another. Eventually, I quit asking. It was no longer worth it. Why would I want to count down the minutes that passed when I wasn't sure which one might be my last?

I have come to learn it is the dead of night when people get more brave. Monsters not only come out at night, but they walk among the living during the light of day. Nightmares, however, are often born in the dead of night and take on a life of their own. Those that suffer at the hands of a monster may choose to let that pain fester until it becomes too much and creates an entity of its own, a nightmare, to survive the only way it knows how when the prey becomes the predator.

Finally, I stumble through the last thicket of branches and emerge from the tree line next to a playground. I check for cars parked along the street or people making their way through the area, but the street is fairly quiet, aside from a young couple on the other side of the playground. Although, late at night or in the predawn early morning hours, anyone you find near a playground is probably far from good news. Then again, they aren't the ones standing naked in a park covered in dirt. I shrug my shoulders at my incessant need to justify everything. Like this is my fault.

Taking a deep pull of air in through my nose, I struggle to exhale it out slowly through my mouth.

"You can do this, Charlie. No problem. So what, some assholes buried you naked and alive in the woods? It could have been worse. You could have been naked and dead. Then what would you have to complain about? Nothing. That's what. You'd be deader than dead," I say as I nod yes to no one but me, convincing myself I'm being completely rational at this moment.

As I walk through the park, I continue to murmur to myself.

I quickly look up to find a couple of teenagers across from me. One gasps like I'm the second coming and the other has his mouth hanging open. I give my best "mean girl stare." I may be a little off because both sets of eyes get a little wider.

"Can I fucking help you?" I snap at the pair. They both shake their heads no. I'm about to continue on my way when I jolt to a stop, realizing I'm still naked and covered in dirt.

"Clothes," I say, holding out my hand as I look at the girl. She sputters and starts backing away.

"I'm not giving you my clothes! Are you crazy?!"

I smile.

And wait.

8

Eventually, her boyfriend removes his clothes. I don't think she likes it too much, but she had her chance. *Jesus.* The look she's giving me. Is this normal? Not only do I not have time for this, but I grew up chained like a prisoner and kept from the outside world. I'm really not even sure what passes for common courtesy or manners. What little I know of the world is usually from overhearing conversations I wasn't supposed to or television shows when I was allowed to watch them.

"Can you hurry? Your girlfriend doesn't seem to like me very much."

I hear a snort come from him, which almost causes me to crack a smile, but this whole situation will have me spinning soon if I don't get my shit together.

I take a quick look around while keeping the couple in my line of sight. You can't be too careful. You never know who you might come across. For example, a naked girl covered in dirt staggering out of the woods and through a park.

Now that I think of it, not once have they asked me if I'm okay, and that makes my temper flare.

"Oh, for fuck's sake, just give me the damn things," I say as I snatch the black joggers out of his hand that were still hanging from one foot as he stepped out of them with the other, leaving him in nothing but boxers.

I pull the black joggers on and roll them down my hips, trying to accommodate my smaller frame. Then, I pull his T-shirt over my head and stick my arms through the holes. As I pull my head through the top, I get a whiff of some sort of cologne or fragrance. It could be worse. It could also be better. Oh well.

Tossing my long tangle of black hair over my shoulder, I mumble a thanks and continue down the road.

9

I do not know where I'm going. I'm not even sure where I am at this exact moment. All I know is that someone just tried to kill me and the only thing I can think of is downing a bucket of ice water to ease this scratchy, raw feeling in my throat.

Chapter Two

Charlie

I'm several blocks away from where I started when I realize the concrete beneath my bare feet is cutting into my skin, causing me to leave a blood trail wherever I go.

I cut through a parking lot and walk around the back of the building looking for the answer to my prayers, and they're answered soon after.

I walk over and notice an older car with all the windows rolled up, press my face against the glass, and spot a pair of flip-flops in the seat.

Aside from my great find of cheap footwear, I realize the situation I'm in now. I want to strangle whatever fucker did this.

I run around the building, bloody feet and all, looking for what I need. After I've found it, I come back to free the small dog.

"Ma'am! Come back here! You need to pay for that!" a man yells from the sidewalk in front of the gas station doors.

"Why? I'm just borrowing it! Besides, you don't even

sell them. This is a gas station!" I huff at him as I continue towards the car.

I go to the opposite side of the vehicle, raise the bat, and swing with all my might into the back passenger window, watching the glass shatter and hoping it doesn't fly in the small animal's direction. I crawl across the glass, not paying attention to the cuts and shards embedding themselves into my skin, and reach first, for the flip-flops, and second, for my newest inconvenience. Because that's exactly what this is. An inconvenience of epic proportions.

This is so unlike me, it's ridiculous. I'm not one of those bleeding heart activists who are all about rescuing every homeless animal, not that I don't think they deserve help, but I'm usually dealing with my own problems and that leaves little time to deal with others. But something about being trapped in the ground gives me a small tinge of sympathy deep, deep down for this dog.

"I seriously don't need this right now, but you caught me in a giving mood," I whisper at the dog. He's looking at me like I'm his new best friend. "Put those eyes away. They won't work on me. But you need a name." I take in the innocent look of the fluffy brown Teacup Maltipoo. At least I think that's what he is, and I don't think they're cheap either. So I'm sure I'm about to piss someone else off.

After double checking that he is in fact a *he*, I finally decide I'll name him later. I need to get going.

I turn around to find a couple of people watching.

"You tell whoever kept this dog locked in the car with no food and water there is a special place in hell for people who mistreat animals," I demand as I slip on my newly gained flip-flops. "And they're lucky it's not hot out or I'd come for them next."

Tossing the bat aside, me and Tea—crap. I think I just

named him. Tea, short for Teacup. Sure. Why not? We carry on down the street. After a few more blocks, I regret not having gone into the gas station for water.

We pass by what looks like a bar but appears more like a hole in the wall. Literally. There's only a small sign that says "BAR" next to a door. I give myself an A-plus for my deductive reasoning skills. Who said I'd never amount to anything?

I push on the door, and it opens. "Come on, Tea. Let's see what kind of trouble we can get ourselves into," I whisper in my new friend's ear. I'm not sure of the time, but the door is open, so in we go.

Walking down the darkened hallway, the scent of sin and cigarettes hits my nose. As we turn the corner, I shield my eyes with one hand while I snuggle further into Tea with my other. These damn lights are killing me. They're not bright by any means, but after walking down the hallway of doom, they're much brighter in comparison.

As my eyes adjust to the lighting, I walk over to the bar, pull my flip-flops off, and toss them on the bar in front of me. Then, I maneuver Tea around to sit in my lap. The poor thing is panting like crazy.

"Can I help you, hun?" a girl, not much older than me, asks from behind the bar while giving me a once over. She's in her early to mid-twenties. Her long dark hair, almost as dark as mine, rests on top of her head in a messy bun. She's wearing a black tank top and white ripped jean shorts.

I watch her as she takes in my appearance in return, sure that it's a lot to take in. Crazily tangled long black hair, flip-flops with bloody feet, sweatpants, and a shirt that's far too large, not to mention the cuts on my arms and hands from climbing across the glass in the car. I'm mostly covered from head to literal toe in dirt from climbing out of the grave

I was buried in. And to top off the look sits a fluffy little dog that can't weigh over ten or fifteen pounds at most. We both look like we could use a bath and a bar of soap.

"Are you okay?" she asks with an unsteady voice.

"I've been walking for what feels like hours and do you know you're the first person to ask me that?" I croak out, and then attempt to clear my throat.

I can see her cringe as she hears my scratchy voice. "Well, you look like you've had a day," she simply states.

I can't help but laugh, finding the humor in her statement. "Oh, I've had a life," I reply. "But this is much better than the way my day started." I take a deep breath to steady myself for the embarrassment I start to feel at my next statement. "I don't have any money. But I would literally kill for a glass of ice water and water for the dog too, please?" I ask while trying my best to give her the sweet innocent eyes look I know I don't have.

I've seen myself in a mirror and am aware enough to admit even I can't see a shred of innocence when I see my reflection. I believe some people have just lived too much and too hard to hold on to such things, and while I may not have lived in an extravagant sense as far as experiences, I've had my fair share of trauma to count as such.

She sighs, then shakes her head and gives a small chuckle. She turns around and makes up an ice water for myself and a bowl of water for Tea, and I can't think of a single thing in this moment that I wouldn't do for this girl. Just this one act of kindness is enough to have me feeling one side of my face lift in a small, barely-there smile. Something I haven't done in years.

She leaves our water in front of us after telling me to let her know if she can get me anything else and walks further down the bar to talk to a man. I can't help but to stare a little longer than what's considered polite when I take in his appearance.

He's older, compared to my twenty years of life. Probably late twenties, early thirties. He has short, cropped, jet-black hair that's longer on top, with stubble along his jawline, and a straight nose with a small bump, as if it had broken one too many times and wasn't set right. He's wearing ripped jeans and a short-sleeve white shirt, tattoos running down his arms, and if I look close enough, I can see he has a small tattoo on the side of his face, right below his temple, of a small spider.

"Well, hello there," I mutter to myself as I take a few gulps of my ice cold water, while attempting to see more of him out of the corner of my eye without appearing too obvious. Tea looks up at me with his big round eyes, as if he understands my words. I'm feeling judged by my new four-legged friend.

"Well hello to you, too, darlin'." I can feel the assault of hot air against my neck that smells of alcohol, giving me severe stranger danger vibes. I got enough of those where I grew up, but I prefer the threat I know to the ones I don't. At least there I knew what to expect. This is my first experience outside of those familiar walls.

I crane my neck away from the bold assailant while attempting to keep the disgust and rage from my face. He steps toward me again, rubbing what little of a bulge he has in his pants against my hip.

"Oh hell no," I murmur under my breath while stepping away from him once again. This time I've had enough, and I walk over to the attractive stranger a few stools down from mine and shove Tea in his direction.

"Hold my dog," I tell him and then abruptly make a

turn and head back in the direction where I was content just moments ago.

Marching up to the man that thought he could rub and grope and breathe on me, I let my temper get the better of me, unable to hold it in anymore.

"Let me tell you something, you limp dick mother-fucker. I may be small. I may look like the little lost girl you think you can take advantage of, but don't let your eyes deceive you. I'm the worst kind of hell you can find. You wanna know why? I just climbed out of a goddamn grave." I can't help but let out a bitter laugh, take a deep breath, then continue on. "You know what that makes me? A fucking zombie. I'll rip your face off with my teeth for fun," I say as I step closer to this asshole, while letting the familiar feeling of rage and thoughts of violence wash over me.

I learned many things growing up in an asylum, including my colorful language skills. I'm not sure if I was born with it. From what I remember of my mother, she mostly just sat there sedated a lot. But *crazy* can definitely be taught, and I had plenty of people to teach me for a while.

"Look what we have here, guys. Little girl thinks she's a badass," he says with laughter in his eyes.

I grab his dick through his pants and twist, then jump up to grab his head and slam it into the bar. He falls to the floor, and I climb on top of him, landing a few punches to his face while seeing red. I then bite his ear and tug with my teeth, ripping a good chunk of it from his head.

Chapter Three

Jax

I see the storm brewing in her eyes as she shoves the little furball in my direction, and I wonder how far this is going to go. She looks like chaos wrapped in damnation. I immediately feel the tension in the air.

"Jax, help that poor girl," Ashlyn whispers loudly in my direction.

"It doesn't look like she needs help to *me*," I say as I grin at my sister, Ashlyn. She swats at my arm.

"Fine. Take the damn mutt," I grumble as I pass the dog off to her and stroll casually toward the inevitable fight that's about to break out between the little terror and the asshole harassing her.

Just as I step forward, I hear her yell some nonsense about climbing out of a grave and something about *zombies* and wonder what the fuck I just got myself into.

The next thing I know, she's slamming his face into the bar and climbing on top of him. I figure I'll let her get a few blows in. After all, he has it coming. But the blows she was raining down quickly turn into what I think was a piece of flesh being spit out of her mouth. I lift my hand and rub my mouth, trying to hide my grin from any bystanders.

Blood is gushing from the side of his head where his ear was only moments ago. She didn't get the whole thing, mostly the earlobe. She sits there in a daze as blood drips down her chin.

"You crazy bitch!" someone yells, while the mangled man wails on the floor, going on about finding his ear. I don't think he realizes he's only missing a piece of it, and I don't even think they sew earlobes back on, but I suppose he'll just have to find that out for himself.

I decide I should probably step in, and walk around the display in front of me, deciding not to approach from behind. I've seen this kind of crazy before. Hell, I *am* this kind of crazy. I know the last thing this little terror needs is to feel like she's being caged in or attacked from behind. I want her to see me when I reach forward to help her off the floor so she's not taken by surprise.

"Come on. Up you go," I say as I lean down to help her up. She swats at my hand and gives me a look that would kill a weaker man. Once she sees it's me and not another friend of her assailant on the floor, her eyes soften a bit, and she lets me help her up.

"Let's get you cleaned up, naughty girl," I say to her as I lead her to the end of the bar, where Ashlyn waits with the girl's dog.

"Charlie," she murmurs as she leans over the bar while wiping her face off with the wet towel Ashlyn handed her. She must see the confusion in my face because she follows that up with a roll of her eyes.

"My name is Charlie," she adds.

"Jax," I say with a grin as I sit back down onto my stool.

Ashlyn slides a fresh cold beer over to me and I take a

swig while keeping Charlie in view. She's a loose cannon. I wonder if she knows it yet, or not. I won't be trusting her anytime soon, that's for sure.

I doubt what she said about climbing out of a grave holds any truth, but she looks like she climbed out of one. I can't argue she doesn't look like that's exactly what happened, because she looks like hell. She's hot. I'll give her that. But it seems like she's been to hell and back...a few times.

Ashlyn comes around to give Charlie back her dog. Another mystery to solve. And Charlie looks surprised to see the mutt. You'd think she would be ecstatic to have him back. I mean, she brought him into a bar with her. If that doesn't scream obsessed, I don't know what does. I'm seriously hoping she's not one of those females who haul their little dog around inside a purse. Nothing against dogs. Love them. But that's just annoying as shit.

"Get over here, Tea. I guess we're stuck together for now." She says to the dog.

"Do you not like your dog or something?" Ashlyn whispers across the bar as if she's afraid to offend her, or the dog. That's not like her at all. She's usually pretty direct. A what you see is what you get, kind of attitude.

"I just found him locked in a car with no food or water. I thought I should jailbreak him. I wasn't really in the right headspace to think that one through. Now he's an inconvenience." She mumbles the last part to herself, almost as if she's disappointed in her lack of self-control.

"You stole a dog?" I ask.

If looks could kill, I'd be dead ten times over after the look she just shot my way.

"I said they locked him in a car with no food or water," she replies.

"So, like I said, you stole a dog," I counter.

"Are you serious right now? The poor dog was all alone, locked in a car with nothing to eat or drink. What if he had to go to the bathroom? Then what? Huh? Would his owner be happy if he peed in the seat? That would probably be a no, asshole."

She continues to talk under her breath to herself, more or less, about not judging unless you yourself have been locked away with no food or water, and I feel myself tense up. I glance over and see Ashlyn's eyes go wide with concern. I don't think that was meant to be spoken out loud for others to hear.

My eyes go back to Charlie, and I take another look at her from a different perspective after removing the metaphorical rose-colored glasses. Her long black hair is tangled and dirty along with her skin, covered in what looks like soil, a vast contrast to the freshly laundered joggers and T-shirt she's wearing. Upon closer inspection, I can see clearly that those clothes are too big for her. She has small scrapes along her forearms, and open cuts on the soles of her feet.

"Charlie, where did you say you were from?" I ask.

"I didn't," she replied. "But since you asked...*hell*."

Chapter Four

Charlie

The Oak Grove Asylum was many things. My personal hell is by far the best description of all, but it wasn't always like that. I didn't realize how different my childhood was from other kids until I could watch television now and then and would see the huge contrast in the lives of TV families compared to my mother's and my own.

I was never told who my father was, but my mother was a patient at the asylum. So it wasn't hard to guess who my father was. Considering she was a patient when she conceived, I had to have been one of the worst-kept secrets inside that place. Though I know there are many.

From symmetrical similarities, it's obvious that Dr. Whitmore was my biological father. Though no one dared to ask. He was the one that took what little freedom I had away and became my jailer.

I was around seven years old when he removed me from my mother's care and dragged me to the small basement on the edge of the property. At first I was locked away, but the more years that passed, the harder I would fight and the worse restrictions I would have to endure, such as not only being locked away, but chained in cuffs. That was after I escaped. *Twice.* Though I didn't get far. Down the hall shouldn't really count as an escape, but it was outside of the basement, so it still counts.

I look at the clock on the back wall and see it's going on almost two in the morning. It's much earlier than I thought it would be. My day is catching up with me. Being drugged and left for dead will do that, I suppose. I'm exhausted and not sure how much longer I will make it on my feet.

Jax is talking, but I honestly have no idea what he's saying. It's all running together, and sounds like I'm in a tunnel. Everything sounds muffled. I go to sit down on the stool next to him, but once I sit, it turns into more of a fall and the last thing I see is the stool I was supposed to be sitting on, falling toward me as I hit the floor and am engulfed in darkness.

I'm LAYING ON SOMETHING WARM AND FLUFFY, WHICH immediately puts me on edge because nothing in my world is soft or comfortable. Jumping up from the couch I was on and falling to the floor, I look for something to defend myself. I have no clue where I am. I catalog the most recent events in my mind. The last thing I was doing was talking to Jax and Ashlyn. I look over and see Jax sitting in the corner on the floor, watching me with a calculative eye, as if I'm some feral animal that might need to be put down.

This is the last thing I need. So I tell him just that.

"No. Don't look at me like that. I've done nothing wrong. Not yet anyway," I add. "Look, I have nowhere to stay. No money. No clothes. Nothing. I wasn't lying when I said I woke up in a shallow grave. I literally dug my way through the dirt to get my next breath. They left me for dead. *Fucking dead,*" I seethe.

"Who left you for dead, Charlie?" Jax grinds out the question as if he doesn't really want the answer.

"It doesn't matter."

"The hell it doesn't! Some chick shows up in my sister's bar talking about climbing out of graves, being a zombie, tearing off ears with her teeth," Jax says.

"Okay, so maybe I'm not a zombie, but that's not the fucking point!"

"Then what is the fucking point?" he yells.

I can't help but roll my eyes as I hold out my wrists for him to take a look at, but he can't seem to see past the dirt covering my arms.

"Look closer," I grumble.

I rub the dirt away that's staining my arms and the bruises around my wrist are becoming more visible than they were only moments ago. It's nearly impossible to miss the angry red, pink and white scarring along with the purple, green, and yellow bruises around my wrists. Some old, some new.

"This is what happens when you're a dirty little secret that needs to be kept. We can't have the good doctor looking like he fucks the patients, now, can we?" I exclaim.

Jax inhales sharply and his eyes become darker by the second.

"Your doctor did this to you?" he asks.

"My father did this to me," I tell him honestly.

Why I feel I can trust a complete stranger is something I don't think I'll ever be able to answer. I just know for whatever reason Jax seems like a protector, and I've never really had one of those. I've never had a friend either. So, I tell him my story. Every dirty detail from my earliest childhood memories, to what I've heard from others at the asylum, to what I experienced at the hands of the monsters within its walls.

He doesn't speak. He just listens. He listens to me lay my soul bare. I remember a story from when I was younger about the Lost Boys. Well, I'm the forgotten girl.

If we put her away, no one will notice. I'm sure that's what they thought when they kept me locked away. Swept to the side and under a rug. I'm not sure why he didn't just put a bullet through my head. That would have been more humane, but humane is not really something they're fond of there.

The more words flow from my mouth, the more anger shifts to the forefront of my thoughts. My father, the doctor. The orderlies. Anyone who helped hide me and *used* me and my mother. How many more patients have they done this to? Just my mother? I didn't see any other children in there. Am I the only one? I have so many questions that need answers.

One way or another, they're all going to pay. *I'll make sure of it.*

"Why are you telling me this?" Jax asks.

"What?" I ask, surprised by his question.

"Are you expecting me to ride in and save the day? Is that what this is, little terror? Am I supposed to feel sorry for you now?"

"Are you serious? You asked for my story, so I gave it to you," I say as I grit my teeth while trying to remain calm.

"No. You're looking for some *white knight* to ride in and save the day. Well, guess what, little girl. No one here is going to do that. I'm not a white knight. I'm the monster from nightmares, not the hero from fairytales."

I can't believe the turn this conversation has taken. I thought I could trust him, and he was someone who would help, but I didn't expect a savior. I know better than to rely on anyone else, much less someone I've just met.

"Do you think I even know what fairytales are? I don't get fairytales. They don't exist in my world. Nightmares *are* my happily ever after. There are no heroes in my story. Everyone is a monster, and the girl saves her damn self. So get off your fucking delusional high horse and shut the fuck up." I snarl at him, the last of my calm demeanor drying up like it was never there to begin with.

This was a mistake. I should have never shared a piece of me with him. *That's what you get, Charlie, for trusting the first attractive male that comes along. He couldn't have been ugly along with being an asshole?* Apparently, the two needed to coincide to make sure I learn my lesson.

Jax storms from the room we're in, and my mind goes into overdrive trying to come up with a solution. It takes less than a minute for me to decide there's only one hand left for me to play.

Chapter Five

Jax

It's the middle of the night and Ashlyn is closing up the bar for the night when I storm from the room, leaving Charlie and her hurt feelings in my wake while I go outside to calm down from the storm brewing inside of me.

I don't really know why I got so mad at her. It wasn't her I was upset with, but the situation she found herself in.

My sister and I had our own problems. A drunk of a father who left his mark on us both, but the night he threatened to sell Ashlyn if I didn't do as I was told, I lost it. He dug his own grave that night ending his reign of terror. It's been me and my sister ever since. Well, and the guys.

Shit. I'm never going to hear the end of this.

I lean against the outside of the building next to the back door of the bar and prop one boot against the wall behind me while I light a cigarette. I inhale and prop my head against the brick wall while looking up towards the night sky. I can clear my head now that I have a little breathing room.

I'm not sure what Charlie wants from me, but I know

it's something. It's human nature to want. Whether she just wants a friend, since I don't believe she's ever had a real one, especially outside of that hospital, or someone that's along for the ride. Hell, even someone to just look out for her. It's something. Someone *always* wants something.

I finish my smoke and head back inside. I make my way to the bar to help Ashlyn clean up for the night. I see she has Charlie's dog in the corner with what looks like a pillow fort.

"What the hell are you doing to this dog?" I ask.

She goes on about her business because she's used to me always complaining about something, and after a few minutes, she replies, "He needed somewhere comfortable to sit while I worked."

I sigh and silently ask myself why I didn't see this coming before. Ashlyn has always wanted a dog, but Dad never let her get one. Not only that, but there was no guarantee it would survive in our household, thanks to him. Then again, Dad didn't survive thanks to me, so there's that.

After helping Ashlyn clean up the bar, I take a seat and rest for a few minutes while she hands me a bottle of water. It's then I realize Charlie has yet to come down from the studio apartment upstairs. It leads right into the bar so there's no way I would have missed her.

Unless...

I take off running up the stairs, taking them two at a time, until I shove myself through the apartment door and start my search for her. If she didn't come down through the bar, there was only one other possibility. She must have left through the back door that opens to a fire escape down the back of the building. We rarely use it, so it's hard to even remember it's there.

The dull ache in my chest for someone I met only a matter of hours ago won't let me forget this one is on me. This is my fault. Part of me wants to say fuck it, she'll be fine, but what does someone who grew up in an asylum, locked away from everyone, know about being fine? I wonder what *fine* is for her.

I search the apartment a second time just to be sure. She was pretty pissed at me, so I wouldn't hold it against her if she's cornered herself off from us right now. But I can only hope, because deep down I know Charlie didn't just take a time out. She ran.

Running seems to be all she knows, but I can't blame her. The system failed her. Kept her locked in a fucking mental institution and no one even knew? Surely someone knew. Somewhere.

Once the system fails you, it's hard to trust anything that comes from the turning cogs of that wheel ever again. It's only a matter of time before they let you down once more. Ashlyn and I learned that early in life, which was why we started taking care of ourselves so young. If our parents didn't look after us, and the government was a laughingstock with getting abused kids out of bad situations, then it was up to us to take care of ourselves.

I guess I see where Charlie was coming from now when she said, *"the girl saves herself."* She was pretty on point with her analogy. If only my ego could have taken the blows with some damn dignity.

I need to quit comparing Charlie to Ashlyn. They're not the same. Charlie's not my sister, thank fuck, because that would get all kinds of complicated on levels I'm not even comfortable admitting to myself yet...or *ever*.

I run back downstairs and search the bar once more. Then I make my way down the shadow lit hallway and out the front door to the street. I look up and down the road, pacing a little each way. I can't find her.

I know she left, but a part of me is holding onto the slightest chance that maybe she didn't. I'm not even sure why, but it looks like it doesn't matter anymore. She's gone. *And she left her damn dog.*

I sit down on the sidewalk and dig my fingers through my hair, brushing it back off of my face and out of my eyes. Now that I know she's not here, I find myself wondering how far she's going to make it. I let out a small chuckle, finding it amusing in a way. After everything she went through, and the little terror gets her feelings hurt and decides running is her best option. Does this girl have even an ounce of survival instinct left in her at all? I went from frustrated because of upsetting Charlie, to livid that she's acting like a child.

I'm thinking I should have been the one in the asylum. Scratch that, we already know that, but this inconsiderate little shit just dumped her fucking dog with my sister, threw a little bitch fit and fucking ran away like a scared little girl. Fuck pissed. I'm fucking furious, and I'm sitting here acting like she was doing *me* a favor by sharing her story with me. Fuck that and fuck her story. Everyone's got one. It doesn't make you special. It makes you a problem.

After trying to calm myself once more, I get up and dust myself off and then head back inside the bar to tell Ashlyn the good news; she gets a new fucking dog.

Chapter Six

Charlie

I walked for at least an hour and couldn't quite get my sense of direction. I know I went through a small town, but it never seemed to end, and everything looked the same. The sun had risen, and I found what looked like an abandoned, decrepit building, and stopped for a break.

What the hell am I doing?

I shouldn't have run. I've never been outside of the asylum. I don't have any money and don't know my way around this town. I have nowhere to go, but instead of pulling myself together and coming up with a plan, I ran.

Some may mistake my running for cowardice, but the truth is I may not have been a patient at the hospital, but I very well should have been. My mother had her set of issues, but I have my very own. Being treated as a prisoner instead of a patient doesn't really afford me the luxury of being diagnosed or being prescribed medication.

If I get overwhelmed with my feelings, I sometimes can't tell what emotion I'm supposed to feel. If something makes me sad or depressed, but I can't identify the feeling right away, it can quickly turn to anger and before I know it, I'm coming down from a rage-filled high with one hell of an emotional hangover and only fragments of memories to piece together.

The staff on my father's payroll were restraining me to a bed long before I realized that wasn't a normal thing to do to a four-year-old. By six years old, I had been through my first round of electroshock therapy, or my father's version of it, anyway. And by the time I turned seven, they could officially label me as a murderer. Well, not officially. That would mean they would have to call the cops and there was no way that was happening with the shady shit going on in that place.

There were staff drugging patients to keep them compliant, not just to make their jobs easier, but to fulfill their sick sexual appetites. One might wonder how a kid learns about sex while in a nuthouse. There's a simple two-word answer. Sex Addicts. Apparently that alone does not warrant a one-way ticket to the nuthouse, but people would be surprised how many mental disorders are diagnosed with a big side of hyper-sexuality disorder. Then, of course, there's the fucked up answer no one wants to hear, that some people truly are just disgusting monsters.

I learned quite a bit from eavesdropping on conversations and therapy sessions before I was locked away. There were even a few who took it upon themselves to teach me things here and there. They cared enough to try and help me learn how to read and write. I like to think it was to give me a fighting chance or maybe it was just to ease their own guilt for not getting me out of there.

AFTER FINDING AN OLD AND BATTERED COUCH IN WHAT appears to be an office in the back of the warehouse, I let myself relax for the first time since I passed out unwillingly back at the bar.

I need to come up with a plan. I've never really met anyone I could call a potential friend that wasn't tied to the hospital with the same constraints as I had been. I tried not to let myself hope for it, but deep down I thought myself lucky for having met two individuals I could see trusting with my secrets.

Maybe it was for the best that I left. I would only bring darkness to their lives. I could sense they already had their fair share of it. Maybe it's intuition or a kindred spirit sort of thing. I guess I'll never know. I have plenty to keep myself busy with for now. That repulsive man who is my biological father, though he would never admit it. The guards he put on my prison doors day in and day out, leaving me at their mercy when he saw fit. Other staff who were responsible for so many horrifying things.

I have some bodies of my own that need to be buried, and I don't plan to stop until they're all in the ground. Every last one of them. I would like to start by finding out who the hell left my mother to rot in that godforsaken asylum in the first place and never came back for her. My memory can be a fickle bitch, but I don't remember my mom ever having a single visitor in all the years I spent with her.

I can't help but wonder if she has family out there. That would mean I have a family too. And if we have family out there, where the hell have they been my entire life? Do they know I exist? If they do, they left me there, and if that's the case, I might need a bigger shovel.

I really need to write this down. The list of names is getting longer by the second.

I'VE HAD WHAT I WOULD CONSIDER TO BE A VERY productive day. I got a bit of rest and then started plotting a few murders. In the grand scheme of things, this is more than I've accomplished in, well, ever.

The sun has already set. It's not too cold, but there's definitely a chill in the air here in the building. There's one large open space when I first walk into the building which is full of cobwebs and covered in layers of dust. The office I lounged in throughout the day was right around the corner in a small room, as if the office was an afterthought. Someone left behind an old scratched up desk and chair along with the vintage couch. The couch is tan and light brown with an even darker brown pattern of leaves and flowers on it, and it has a suede or velvety touch but uncomfortable wooden arms on each end. It's hideous actually. Brown on top of brown on top of brown. But an old ugly couch is better than no couch at all. I can sleep anywhere as long as it's not my former residence.

I walk around scoping out the place a bit more and see there are a couple of other empty rooms filled with dust along with two bathrooms. One bathroom has a shower setup inside. As if whoever owned the building or worked here before practically lived here themselves. The other bathroom simply has a toilet and sink.

I haven't had a drop to drink all day and my sore throat

is paying for it now. I reach down and turn the handle. As I hear the faucet trickle with the sound of water flowing freely, I breathe a deep sigh of relief for the fact I will have running water to drink, while I block out the familiar feeling of dread and painful memories the sound also brings along. I lean down and place my mouth under the faucet, taking in large gulps of water as it pours out.

After I quench my thirst, I remove my clothes that were only given to me last night to wear and step into the shower after adjusting the temperature. The water isn't too warm, but I'm thankful to be breathing and standing under a working faucet.

I can't even remember the last time I had a shower or bathed in any sense of the word. It had been weeks since I was allowed near any water at all, unless they gave it to me in a small paper cup.

I look around and don't find any soap. I'll deal with that later. For now, I can at least rinse the dirt and blood from my skin and the soles of my feet, along with any small shards of glass that may still be left in my hair or the cuts on my arms.

I stayed in the shower long after the water had turned cold. The skin on my fingers had shriveled up like raisins from the time I had spent under that glorious waterfall. Cold water be damned.

I put the joggers back on after I exited the shower, along with the T-shirt that ran a couple sizes too big. Some people may not think much of this outfit, but to me, it was like Christmas. Not the kind of Christmas we had at the asylum, but the kind of Christmas you see on one of those television shows where there are presents under a ridiculously decorated tree and they leave cookies and milk out.

I'll never understand how they could waste perfectly

good food on a strange man breaking into your home to check on little kids who bribes them with toys. Santa should totally be on the sex offender registry, a naughty list of his own making, if he's not already. Just my two cents. The creepy fuck.

I'm getting hungrier by the minute and have no money for food, but I can at least try to earn some to pay for things like food and anything else I might need until I come up with a better plan. As I walk on the side of the road in search of a gas station or restaurant, I try to come up with a cover story for this mess of a life I'm living right now.

For obvious reasons, I can't go around telling anyone who will listen that someone tried to kill me, and I've grown up chained in the basement of said asylum by the doctor, who also just happens to be my father.

They would for sure make one phone call and send me right back to that fucking place. I've tried the truth, and it got me a big fat fuck you, and not the kind I'd ever hope to get from a man like Jax.

I need to come up with something believable. Not that I want anyone to feel sorry for me, but realistically I would have a better chance if my lie held a bit of truth. With that in mind, I try to wipe the small grin from my face as I approach the small diner up ahead.

Chapter Seven

Jax

My thoughts have been on an endless loop since Charlie left yesterday. I can't help but feel partly responsible for that. If what she said held any truth, she had been through more than even I could understand, and I at least had my sister, Ashlyn. The guilt is piling up on my conscience tonight, and I couldn't shake it.

Is she still alive? Did they realize she survived and go after her?

I've spent the day driving up and down these streets looking for anyone that fits her description, and while I have run into a few younger girls with long black hair, they weren't Charlie. Not even close once I got a better look.

She somehow climbed under my sister's skin almost as much as she had mine. Ashlyn has been giving me the third degree ever since I went back inside last night, or early this morning, from searching the street in front of the bar for Charlie after she ran off.

She's like that. *We* are like that. We have a few friends

we met growing up along the way, and we're more like a small dysfunctional family than anything else.

The truth is, I try to give Ashlyn whatever she wants. I spoil my sister. She doesn't ask for much, so when she asks, it's usually for a reason. This time she wants her new adopted BFF back. How the hell she became that over just a few hours when it was me Charlie mostly talked to, I have no idea, but here we are. And fine. I might be using that as an excuse to ease my own guilt and need to find her.

WALKING THROUGH THE DOOR, I HEAR THE BELL CHIME above my head. I don't wait for anyone to seat me and continue on my way to the back corner booth. I don't come in here a lot anymore, but I used to, when I was younger.

I slide in and grab the menu that's wedged between the napkin dispenser and salt and pepper shakers. I haven't been to Sonny's Diner in forever, but aside from a few new updates to the fifties style decor, everything is pretty much the same. Including the food on the menu, which is good considering they have a chili cheeseburger and crinkle cut fries that are worthy of undying loyalty. It's in that moment I make a vow to myself that I will come back more often.

I continue to look over the menu to see if anything else has changed, as I hear scuffling shoes approach and a pen click. Not thinking anything of it, I place my order while I flip through the menu.

After realizing how engrossed I must have been instead of showing common courtesy and looking at the server while they take my order, I put the menu back in its rightful place and glance up only to see I'm once again alone with my thoughts; the server having left a while ago, most likely to put my order in.

I glance up and look out the window beside my booth, which has a view of the sidewalk and parking lot in front of the diner. I can't help but let my thoughts run wild while thinking of Charlie and wondering where she might be by now. I'm hoping she hasn't gotten herself into any more trouble than she's already in.

For a moment, I think I must be hallucinating as I see her reflection in the window I'm looking out of. I realize it's not on the outside, but on the inside. I turn my head so fast I should probably be concerned about giving myself whiplash.

I look up and feel a small smirk try to pull at the corner of my mouth, but the look on her face has me shutting it down so fast I never would have known it was there to begin with.

Her expression has me questioning exactly how I must have talked to her the last time we were in the same room together. Her eyes are red rimmed and filling with tears, but not quite full enough to fall over the edge of her lids and down her face.

I'm about to apologize when Sonny herself comes up to the table and smacks me on the back of my head. The woman might be in her seventies, but she's feisty as fuck. I can see that hasn't changed.

"Hey, Sonny," I mumble as I rub the back of my head and wonder what the hell that was for. I look up and see Charlie's eyes spark for only a moment, so fast that it's gone before I can fully understand what it was.

"Don't you hey me, boy," Sonny scolds me as her brows dip low.

"I been here how many years now?" she asks.

49

I start to reply, but before I get a word out, she starts again.

"Too long. That's how long. Long enough to witness something I ain't ever seen. Something I didn't think I ever *would* see, *Jaxton Jameson Jagger*," she says with a sass only she and my sister have ever fully been able to pull off when it comes to me.

Aw hell. She *full named* me.

Shit.

I glance over her shoulder to look for Charlie, hoping we can have a moment to talk, when Sonny pops me on my nose with a menu like a damn dog with a newspaper.

"Eyes on me, boy," she says with a warning.

"Yes, ma'am," I reply on autopilot with the same words she ingrained in me and my sister growing up.

"Now I know you, Jax. Jaxton Jameson Jagger don't mistreat no girls. Not a one. None that don't deserve it, anyway," she says with a snicker and then quickly clears her throat to cover it.

I can't help but chuckle.

"So tell me why I got a girl coming up in here with cuts and bruises and bloody damn clothes with no food, needing money to eat or a job to earn some money, and when I ask her where she came from the first name out her mouth was yours." She delivers the statement as facts while using her fingers to list off each item.

What the ever loving fuck is going on here?

"Now let's all just calm down." I try to reason.

Nope. wrong damn thing to say. Don't tell a woman to calm down. They definitely will not do that. At all.

"What I'm trying to say is that you know me, Mrs. Sonny. I would never do anything like that," I explain.

"Now I ain't sayin' you did, boy," she says with a hint of regret.

I know this woman. I can tell she's not accusing me of anything, but simply warning me to watch myself.

It's obvious now what's happened, and I can't decide if I want to stab someone or bend Charlie over my knee and give her a damn well deserved spanking for putting the closest thing to a mother-figure me and Ashlyn have into the middle of our mess.

Her mess.

Fuck.

AFTER THE HEATED AND AWKWARD ENCOUNTER AT THE diner, I went back to the bar and gave Ashlyn the rundown on what had transpired. She couldn't help but laugh in my fucking face. *Perfect.*

Her next course of action was to invite Charlie here tonight and give her the warm welcome she should have been given the first night we met. Things I didn't even consider, like a place to stay, clothes, food, and all necessities.

It was the least I could do after making her the scape-goat for my latest round of paranoia causing her to run off because I lost my temper and raised my voice at her. My childhood never strays too far from my mind. The sense of self-preservation winning out time and time again.

Everything that transpired tonight made one thing abundantly clear. My little terror likes to play games. She's a survivor through and through, doing whatever it takes to see another day.

The girl climbed out of a literal grave. If that's not a survivor move, I don't know what is.

Chapter Eight

Charlie

Ashlyn picked me up from the diner tonight, where Mrs. Sonny had hired me under the table, whatever that means. I just knew I got money to buy things with, while she got to keep a close eye on me. It was a win-win for everyone involved, really.

I had no idea that Jax and Ashlyn knew Mrs. Sonny, but how would I? I took a risk leading my sob story in Jax's direction and then deflecting when she was looking for solid accusations. We both knew I wasn't trying to get him in any trouble, and she seemed to respect that even though I embellished my tale here and there, I didn't outright lie to get him in trouble.

Ashlyn set me up in her bathroom as soon as we got back to her apartment above the bar. After I had thoroughly scrubbed myself from scalp to toe, she had me change into the outfit she picked out for me and then did my hair and makeup.

I had never worn makeup. I didn't count the times I had rummaged through other patients and even some nurses' belongings and stole a lipstick here or an eyeshadow there. I was too young then to even know how to apply it. I only knew that when they wore it, other people seemed to like them more, and I wanted people to like me too.

Stupid me. I did not know what that meant at the time.

"Okay. Take a look," Ashlyn orders excitedly.

I have no idea what to expect. I figure I'll let her have her fun for now, and I can always wash it off if it's just not my style, assuming I can figure out what my style is in a single night.

I climb off the ottoman at the foot of her bed and walk over to the full-length mirror she has attached to the inside of the closet door that stands open.

I open my eyes and can't help the gasp that quickly escapes my lips. I see my eyes widen in the mirror as this stranger stares back at me. The barrage of emotions leaves me feeling slightly off kilter.

While it feels like a stranger staring back at me in the mirror, it also doesn't. It is starting to feel like I'm finally seeing on the outside what and who I feel I truly am on the inside.

I don't know why Ashlyn owns a bar, but she could have become some sort of stylist or makeup artist I'm pretty sure.

The hair took a lot longer than I had expected, but it was completely worth it. My long black mane is now a vibrant purple, but still somehow has held onto a hint of black depending on the lighting.

She had asked me what my favorite color was before I got in the shower earlier and I told her how I read that purple represents transformation. It was a lie. I had actually overheard someone say that in a therapy session and I was hoping like hell that it was actually a fact, but that was a little embarrassing to admit to, so I stuck with my version of the truth. Close enough, but in this moment, I honestly could have cared less because it looked...beautiful, in a way.

Free. It makes me feel free.

After finally moving on from the shock and awe of the purple hair, the next thing I notice is the makeup she had applied. She had given me what she called a light smokey eye, which now made total sense with its smoky, charcoal color.

She had gone light on the eyeliner and used nothing else aside from the lightly tinted lip gloss. She had me pick my favorite out of three and I chose this one simply because it smelled like coconuts.

I did not know what coconuts smelled like, but I never expected them to smell so good. They looked like big hairy balls that were white and milky on the inside from what I had seen and read, and I just didn't see how that seemed very appetizing. But when I smelled the lip gloss, it was definitely the one I wanted her to use.

Apparently, there was a reason for all the hype.

"Well?" Ashlyn asked.

I jolt from her voice, unaware that I had been staring at myself for who knows how long, and continued my perusal, moving down to my outfit. I loved it when it was laying out for me to try on, but I love it even more now that I can see myself in it. It felt like me.

I am wearing a black short-sleeved T-shirt with the white outline of roses that appeared to make up a heart with the word envy embedded in the middle, topped with a black leather jacket.

My jeans are black and ripped at the knees, and my shoes are black lace-up boots.

I am completely in love with the new me, but I can't

help the small whisper in the back of my mind hoping Jax might someday be too.

Ridiculous. What even is that?

I quickly crush the silent hope I was entertaining in my head and turned around, throwing my arms around Ashlyn, and hugging her like I had never hugged someone, *anyone*, before.

I couldn't help the single tear that slid from my watering eyes and I quickly swiped it away, hoping it was gone before she could notice.

"Thank you," I murmur into her hair as I continue to give her a hug. I was new to this hugging thing, and it was painfully obvious if the grunt she let out was anything to be concerned with.

I jump back in concern as she let out a small laugh and we both smiled. My smile being the first real one I had given freely in years.

"You look beautiful," she compliments.

"I feel beautiful. Thank you," I replied.

"No need to thank me, Charlie. You're a badass chick. You just needed the look to match the attitude," she says.

I feel it. Another smile. I can't help but wonder how many more would appear before the night was over.

Chapter Nine

Jax

The guys were already here when I got back from the diner earlier tonight. I tried to tell Ashlyn how everything went down with Sonny, but it was damn near impossible to do without them overhearing.

Turns out I didn't need to worry. They had already heard every bit of mine and Charlie's chaotic encounter from Ashlyn by the time I walked back through these doors.

I keep nothing from them, so they knew I would have told them. They just didn't know when. And right now, the when was the key. Because tonight was not the night for what they had planned. I could see it in their eyes.

There is too much craziness going on between Charlie and me. I was honestly hoping to just chill and talk some things out, but it looks like other plans are being made and she's not even aware of them yet.

I can't help the electric charge that I suddenly feel flowing through my veins.

Excitement. We haven't had any in a while. Not the kind I'm sure we're about to be in for.

Charlie may not know it yet, but she's about to get her wish granted. Whether she knows it's what she wished for or not.

I'M LEANING OVER THE POOL TABLE WITH CUE IN HAND, lining up to sink the eight ball for a win, when I notice my boys' heads snap in the same direction simultaneously and I know what they've seen.

While I know they can't help it, because I sure as fuck can't either, I really wish I could crack this stick across the back of their necks. She's not theirs to look at.

She's not yours either, asshole.

Realizing I can't resist the pull myself, I lay down the cue and step around the table while following their line of sight and where it leads. Charlie and Ashlyn are both standing at the end of the bar talking.

Fuck me.

Nope. No way.

This time, instead of imagining it, I turn around and smack the one closest to me in the back of the head, channeling the pop Mrs. Sonny gave me earlier tonight to get him to shut this shit down.

One look at me and the look in my eyes and he knows. The sooner he gets the others on board, the sooner we can move on from it.

I decide in this very moment that if I'm going all in on this, I'm doing it my way.

I stroll across the bar and slide up beside Charlie while she's talking to my sister. This new look of hers, the word beautiful, doesn't even begin to cover it.

"You look gorgeous. You know that, right?" I ask.

"Well, thanks," Charlie replies with a bit of shock in her voice.

"You were gorgeous before, but the difference now is that you look like you *know* it. That's a *good* thing, little terror," I say quietly.

Her jaw seems to hit the floor, and a moment later she hands me my ass.

"Jaxton Jameson Jagger, are you flirting with me?" she asks teasingly, and loudly.

"Fuck," I mumble. "Did you just full name me, too?"

"You *do* realize your name sounds like a mix of a porn star and a rock star, don't you?" she asks incredulously.

I suddenly hear laughter around us and notice the guys have made their way over from the pool tables in the back.

For the first time since I started talking to her tonight, her attention moves away from me, and I'm not sure I like it.

Yeah. Definitely don't like it.

"What would you know about porn stars and rock stars anyway?" I ask curiously.

"No one censored their language where I grew up. I learned all sorts of things kids probably shouldn't at a young age."

Ashlyn catches Charlie's attention again and is going to introduce her to our friends, but being the asshole that I am, I jump in to take over to make sure everyone here knows their place.

Charlie. Mine. For example.

"This is Liam, Wren, and Kai." I name them off as I point down the bar they've gathered around.

Looking back at them, I drape an arm over Charlie's shoulder and lean down towards her ear while holding eye contact and speaking to them. "This is Charlie," are the words that flow slowly from my mouth, but what they hear is what I want them to hear. That she's off the fucking table, because like I said, whether she knows it, she's fucking mine. That's just the way it's going to be.

EVERYONE BUT CHARLIE AND ASHLYN HAS HAD AT least a couple drinks tonight. I cut myself off a while ago because I was not thinking and forgot that while this girl was a prisoner; it also sheltered her from the world of mundane things we take for granted, like alcohol tolerance.

I don't think she's ever even had an actual beer before until tonight. So we thought it best to stop her after one. For tonight, at least. I don't think she liked it, anyway. She seemed like she could not care less. Probably for the best. One less demon for her to have to fight.

I had planned to apologize for the way things had gone down with us before, but I didn't really want to go into the details in front of a bar full of people. I'll save that for later tonight, or tomorrow, if she's still around.

Chapter Ten

Charlie

I smile and play the part he apparently expects me to fit right into. The angry but clueless girl who knows nothing of the outside world. It's effortless really. The way it almost feels like he crafted it just for me.

There are a few things going on here that he doesn't seem to understand. I haven't forgotten the way he yelled at me after I bled my heart out to him like a naïve fool. That's normally not something I would do.

I could blame it on the events that had occurred over the last forty-eight hours, or I could just call it like it is. A mistake. Pure and simple.

He came across as if he cared and I couldn't fathom why a stranger would care, so I took a chance. A chance that proved me wrong.

He witnessed part of my crazy. There's no putting it back in the box. So, he either thinks it was a one off because of the situation, or he just doesn't care as long as crazy comes in a nice little package. After the way he behaved tonight in front of their friends, he seems to think everything is just fine between us.

Maybe I'm not the only crazy one here.

I talked to Ashlyn, and she told me I could sleep in the spare room in her apartment upstairs tonight. With everything I've gone through recently, I have had little sleep and I can feel my body trying to warn me I need to take a step back. I really don't want exhaustion to welcome me with open arms the way it did the first night I was here, so I head upstairs and into the room she showed me to earlier in the night.

I slip out of the clothes she had given me to wear and into the long T-shirt that was thrown across the bed haphazardly.

The scent on this shirt isn't Ashlyn's, and it's a far cry from the scent that was on the one I had taken from the last guy. I recognize this one though. It smells like *him*, and I can't help but wonder what it's doing here.

I try to turn off my thoughts and let my mind go blank as I climb onto the bed and under the covers. It's hard for me to do that though. If my instincts are telling me to stay alert even as I'm unconscious, then that is what I will do.

I must have just started to doze off if only for a moment because I didn't hear anyone come into the room, but I hear his perfect lips calling my name like it was always meant to roll off his tongue in the most delicious way.

Snap out of it, Charlie.

I pop one eye open to see where he is in the room. As I look around, I notice the dark silhouette on the chair in the corner of the room. I know it's him.

"I know you're awake," he whispers.

I can't help but roll my eyes at his arrogance.

"What?" I snap.

I hear him sigh loudly before he continues on.

"I just wanted to apologize for the other night. That was a shit thing for me to do," he admits softly.

I can't help the small laugh that escapes me, but he remains silent. *Waiting.*

"Do you honestly think that saying you're sorry is going to take back everything you said to me? The way you treated me? Do you understand how you made me feel?" I ask.

"I've told no one my story. *No one.* And the one time I decide to open up, you make me feel like an idiot. The first person I met outside of the hell I lived in my entire life. But that's okay. I mean, who am I? I'm no one. I didn't come here to give you a sob story, or whatever you want to call it, if that's what you're thinking. I just thought you seemed like someone who would understand. Maybe I was wrong. Maybe what I thought I saw in you was nothing more than a simple-minded boy who likes to act like he can fill the shoes of a grown man."

"That's a bit of a low blow, don't you think? Coming from a girl who just showed up the way she did. Cut me a little slack here, Charlie. Come on. You looked crazy," Jax exclaims.

"Don't call me crazy. Whether I am or not is none of your damn business," I say as I feel the need to defend myself.

"Hold on. That's not what I'm trying to say. I'm fucking this all up," Jax says with a sigh.

"What I mean is, you came in here looking the way you did. I understand that guy was in the wrong and he deserved what you gave him, but coming from a girl who walks into a strange place and doesn't know anyone, who then gets in a fight, and then talks about climbing out of graves while covered in scratches and blood and glass toting a pint-sized dog? I was just thinking it seemed so bizarre and crazy at the time. That it was just too much and I'm sorry. That wasn't fair to you," Jax explains.

"You're right. That was not fair to me, but you're also right about everything else," I say quietly as I roll over in the bed so that I can see him better in the dark from where I lay.

"I have to admit though, the last thing I expected you to do was run. You didn't really seem like a runner to me. You are someone I would think would stay and fight. Hell, you *did* fight. So the last thing I expected was for you to run because of something I said," Jax says.

"Oh, don't flatter yourself. I didn't run because of what you said. Not because it hurt my feelings, but because I was afraid of what I might do. You pissed me off. I was mad. I can't always control the things I say or do when I get mad. I didn't want to hurt you. Okay? The way you and Ashlyn treated me was the nicest I had been treated in a long time, if ever. Especially from complete strangers. So when I got mad, I didn't want to stay around and say something I would regret or do something I couldn't take back. The next best thing for me to do was to run. So I did, and I will not apologize for it. I probably should, but I needed that time to cool off, and you obviously needed time to get your head on straight. That's kind of rich coming from me," I say as I mumble the last sentence.

"I really am sorry, Charlie. I never meant to make you feel like shit. Can you forgive me?" Jax asks.

"Fine. I guess I can forgive you. It's not like anybody else is crazy enough to let me hang around," I say with a laugh.

"Who said I was going to let you hang around?" Jax asks with a smile.

"Come on! You like me. You know you like me. I'm a likable person," I gloat.

"Not saying you're not. I actually agree with you on that and under different circumstances, I'd like to think we would have started off on a completely different note," Jax states.

I can't help but let out a relieved sigh.

"Don't go getting soft on me, Jaxton Jameson Jagger," I say with a playful smile.

"Do I look soft to you?" Jax asks with a chuckle.

The playful banter is a nice reprieve from our usual ranting back and forth and foaming at the mouth with rage, but it also makes it hard for me to know how I should take that question. So instead of attempting to flirt, which I'm painfully aware I have no practice doing, I stretch and fake a yawn.

Chapter Eleven

Jax

I scoot to the edge of my chair and lean forward with my elbows on my knees, watching the little terror act like she has no interest in me. I guess we'll see about that.

I wait a few minutes and when she says nothing else to me or doesn't move in the slightest; I stand on my feet and slowly make my way across the room toward her.

After everything she's been through, the last thing I want is for her to feel alone. I have yet to ask her where she stayed last night, but I'm sure Ashlyn will fill me in later. I walk to the opposite side of the bed and slide off my shoes, then slowly climb in next to her so as not to move her too much if she somehow truly fell asleep in the last few minutes.

I lay on my side and scoot closer. Placing my hand on her hip, I turn her away from me, wrap my arm around her with my hand pressed to her stomach, and pull her back toward me as the little spoon to my big one.

Without thinking, I turn and press my lips to her hair, kissing her head as if this is something I do every night.

To my surprise, she shuffles back into me, bringing us closer together, and the next words that come from her mouth are both terrifying and satisfying in equal measure.

"I have plans. Big, bloody plans," she whispers.

"Oh yeah?" I ask.

"Mmhmm. I spent the day yesterday making a list."

"You did, huh? Tell me who's on your list, little terror," I murmur into her hair.

And so she does.

She rattles off names and for those she doesn't have a name for, I tell her how we can get them, which gets her even more excited.

Before I know it, she's rolled over and is now facing me. She threads her legs through mine and starts braiding strands of her long, now purple hair, while I listen to her "bloody plans."

I catalog what I can in my mind for future reference, should the need arise. I'm sure it will. This girl has had time to think and plan, and not just yesterday. I'm pretty sure she spent most of her time locked away planning what she would do should she ever find herself free of that place. And who wouldn't?

"Ashlyn told me some things about how the two of you grew up," she says quietly.

"Did she?" I ask.

I'm not surprised, and I honestly don't hold it against my sister. I'm glad she feels she can talk to Charlie. She doesn't really have anyone that understands her the way I do. The way I'm sure Charlie does.

We have the guys. They're like family to us. But I try to keep Ashlyn out of a certain business with them unless it's absolutely necessary for her to be in the know about a situation. If something could put her in danger, then I'll bring her into the circle. Her safety comes first.

"I feel like you see me. *Me*." She whispers.

"I know I do. I think that's why I got so pissed after you told me your story. It felt like living mine all over again. Definitely different circumstances, but the pain is the same. I could feel it in my bones. Feel *you* in my bones."

She goes silent for a few seconds as we sit in the dark room and the next thing I know; I feel her lips press against mine.

She jerks back suddenly, not only surprising me, but herself. I caress her cheek with the palm of my hand as gently as I can and guide her slowly back down to press my lips against hers once again.

She eagerly strokes her tongue against mine as I wrap my arms around her body and roll her on top of me.

I'm not sure how fast or how slow to go with her because of her past, but it seems I don't have to know.

She sits up and straddles my lap, pressing her heat that's covered by a thin piece of fabric against the rigid length growing inside my jeans. I let out a small growl as she lifts her shirt, *my shirt*, over her head, along with any bra that may have been covering her perky round tits.

She rocks back and forth, searching for relief from the friction she's creating between us, and releases an erotic breathy moan that has what little control I have left breaking.

I reach up and pull her down to my chest once again and flip us over so that she's on her back as I press myself between her legs.

"Do you have any idea how fucking gorgeous you are?" I ask as I bend down and take her nipple between my teeth and give it a teasing tug.

She squirms as she presses her chest further into my mouth.

"Fuck," she says in a breathy tone.

"Harder."

My eyes dart up to hers. I want to make sure I heard her correctly.

She's staring back at me as she nods her head yes.

"Please," she begs.

"You're a dirty girl. Aren't you, baby?" I tease.

She whimpers while trying to press harder into me.

"I thought you might be," I add.

I give her nipple a nice firm tug as I grip the thin strip of her underwear and simultaneously tug on those as well, feeling them break free.

"Please," she pleads again.

I pepper kisses along her stomach and waist as I make my way down further between her legs until I come face to face with perfection.

I slowly lick up and down each side of her mound, avoiding the bundle of nerves she's so desperately trying to get me to strike with my tongue. I lean back and take in the sight of her arousal, then thrust two fingers inside her glistening pussy.

"Is this what you want? You want your pussy fucked?" I ask.

"Yes!"

"Yes what?"

"Yes please!" she begs loudly.

"Good girl."

I can feel her grow even more wet with those two simple words of praise.

I continue to thrust my fingers back and forth inside her as I lower my face back down and dart my tongue out to stroke her clit. She can't help but to rock up and down my face. She wants more, and that's what I intend to give her.

In a moment faster than either of us expects, I have us flipped around with me on my back and I pick her up by the waist and drop her right where I want her.

"Ride my face, little terror. Take what you want."

She rocks frantically back and forth over my tongue, her juices dripping onto my face and rolling down my chin. I don't think I've ever tasted something so sweet.

I slip two fingers inside her pussy to fuck her again while I use my other hand to hold on to her hip and grind her down harder into my face.

"You feel so good," she says as she pants inconsistently.

I help her pick up speed and am rewarded shortly after when I feel her pussy tighten around my fingers.

"Give it to me, baby. All of it," I reply. Moments later, a gush of liquid rushes into my mouth and is dripping along my chin and down my neck. I continue to suck the nectar from her core as she jerks and slows her pace above me.

She falls to the side of me and instead of us getting up to clean ourselves off; she scoots herself back against me and I hold her once again as we both fall into slumber much easier than I have in a very long time.

Chapter Twelve

Charlie

This is incredible. The sun shining down today is a nice warm welcome considering I haven't ever spent much time under its golden rays in the past. I hold my arms out to my sides and try to lean my head back to enjoy the sun and the breeze until Jax reaches his arm behind him and I'm unceremoniously slapped across my thigh in warning.

Oops. I guess that's not allowed.

Apparently, he has a motorcycle. I'm not sure if he was on one when he came to the diner the other day. I don't think I heard a bike pull up, but I could be wrong.

We're on our way to meet up with Kai, Liam, and Wren. Jax informed me this morning of what he does for a living. Contract killer.

Why do I find that so hot?

He mentioned the guys, but didn't want to go into too much detail because he wouldn't want them telling his business to other people, and they wouldn't, so he wants to afford them the same respect.

W<small>E PULL UP TO WHAT LOOKS LIKE A COMPOUND</small> fenced in with a gated entrance. They must be expecting us because as we approach the gate, it slides open.

I don't notice the sign until we're almost past it, and even then I only catch a glimpse. Wicked *something* MC. I can't make out the second word.

Oh well.

We pull around to the side of the building and Jax parks the bike. After helping me off, he takes my helmet, hanging it on the handlebars and takes my hand in his as we're greeted by a door opening and Wren flagging us to come inside.

"Hey, man," Jax says as we walk through the door.

"Brother," Wren replies in greeting as he pulls ahead and leads us through the building, while nodding his head at me in passing.

I'm not sure if the gate outside is to keep people in or keep them out, possibly both. It reminds me of the asylum in that way, so I don't feel very comfortable traipsing through the place like I belong here when I clearly don't.

Wren leads us into a room after entering an access code into a panel beside the door. I can't help but think that this seems like some crazy spy shit, which has me smiling from ear to ear. Jax notices and lets out a small chuckle while Wren gives me a curious look as we approach Liam and Kai.

If I thought a keypad was impressive, it's got nothing on the room full of computers we walk into.

We all take a seat as Jax tells them the information required to help us get some answers from my past.

After a few hours, Jax seems to think we have everything we need to get started with my plans. We say our goodbyes and get back on the road.

I step into the room and the first thing I see is a wall covered in computer screens.

"Security cameras," Jax says from behind me as he's pressed against my back, rubbing both of my arms up and down.

I tilt my head to the side to look up at him. His tall frame should intimidate me, but I find I rather like it. Just imagining the things we could do...

I feel my back vibrate as I snap out of my daydream to notice Jax trying to hold in the laughter that shines so easily through his eyes, causing his chest to rumble against me from behind.

"I would love to see what images you have flashing through your mind right now. If that look in your eyes is any indication, they're naughty as fuck," he says with humor and lust in his tone.

I can't help the smirk that pulls from the corner of my mouth as I turn and step further into the room.

"Is this your Batcave?" I ask.

"My Batcave?"

"Yeah. You know. The hero has a home base or whatever."

"I'm no hero, little terror. I'm the villain," he states with certainty.

"Good. Villains are more fun anyway."

I continue to walk further into the room and past the monitors. I look around at the weapons he has on display and can't help but feel a vibration deep inside me. I've heard people say they felt like they had butterflies in their stomach, but this feels more like a swarm of bees buzzing in mine.

Just imagining what we could do with these, the possibilities are endless.

"What's it going to be?" he asks.

I look around once again and settle on the easiest, but oddly tempting, section of knives.

"Good choice."

"Well, it's not like I know how to shoot a gun," I mumble with disappointment.

"True. Grab what you want."

I go around the shelves until I find a leather belt. It's overly thick. Too wide to be a belt and has too many straps. More than I could initially see at first glance. Then I notice there are five empty slots. Jax must see my confusion.

"They hold knives," he informs me.

"Sold."

He laughs at my comment and grabs the knives and adds them to their rightful place in the pockets of the straps.

"Now this hooks over one shoulder and goes diagonally across your chest, landing on your opposite hip," Jax says as he straps my weapon of choice onto my body.

"How does that feel?"

"Like I'm about to fuck some shit up," I say with a straight face.

He can't help but laugh as he continues to pack away

some things for himself. Things I'd love to get my hands on. A gun, knife, wait. *Was that a grenade?*

I probably shouldn't be this excited, but when I was little, I would imagine what it would be like to get gifts at Christmas and if I had to attach a feeling to Christmas, this would be it. Bees buzzing in my tummy with grenades and pointy objects that make people bleed.

He finishes packing up and turns me to face him, grabbing my face with both hands.

"If anything goes wrong, you come back here," Jax says as he presses his forehead against mine.

"Nothing is going to go wrong."

"Promise me, Charlie."

"What? I thought I was crazy, but you're acting like *you* are the one who should be medicating," I say with snark, not appreciating that he thinks I won't be able to pull this off.

"Just...promise me."

"Fine. Fuck! I promise. Happy?"

He gives me a cocky grin then leans in and presses his lips to mine.

I can't help but think back to last night and everything that happened between us.

Was I surprised he apologized? Not really. He may come across as arrogant, but even with the rough around the edges demeanor he gives off, he can't help but let a little sugar fall through the cracks.

What I was surprised about however, was the fact that I took it upon myself to shove my tongue down his throat. He probably can't figure out what's up or down with me and my situation.

I hate the word. I hate to even say it. *Rape.* It makes me feel weak and dirty. It shouldn't. The word itself isn't dirty. It's the people who are responsible for the act that are the monsters. The ones who take and take until there's nothing left, but...well...*me*.

Growing up, I was raped repeatedly by whoever either found their way on their own to the basement where I was locked away or by whoever was told to find me specifically.

It wasn't constant. I lost track of time down there, but I do know that months went by sometimes where I was never even touched at all. That wasn't always the case though.

Eventually I started to go along with it. I won't apologize for that. I was breaking and I'll be damned if he was going to break me. So I tried to convince myself I could play along. It made them want me less, but it didn't stop them.

I gave up on that toward the end of my being there though. It wasn't working and I was making myself sick trying to convince myself I didn't care. Instead, the last thing I remember was fighting like hell to stop someone from using my body as if it were theirs to use in the first place.

If not for all of that, Jax would have been my first kiss. He still is my first *real* kiss and not one that was forced. I can't help but hope he doesn't think less of me because of that.

"You still with me?" Jax asks as he snaps his fingers in front of my face.

"Just thinking. Sorry."

"Do you know who you want to pay a visit to first?" he asks.

There's that feeling again. Bees buzzing in my tummy.

"I know who," I reply with a satisfied smile.

This should be fun.

Chapter Thirteen

Jax

Before we left the cabin I gave Charlie a burner phone and a crash course on how to use it and saved mine and Ashlyn's numbers along with the guys in case she needs it for anything. I also made sure she had plenty of cash in the event that we should get separated for any reason and she needs to make her way back to the cabin, which also doubles as a safe house for me.

I know she thinks I'm going overboard, but doing this for as long as we have, you learn that you need to make these plans in case shit doesn't go down the way you expect it to.

I just hope that doing this is everything she hopes it will be. I want her to get her vengeance, and we both know if she was kept in that hell her entire life and no one ever reported it, someone is in bed with law enforcement. No surprise there. Too bad for them they're about to get fucked harder than they probably thought possible.

"We're almost to town. Who's first?" I ask.

Charlie pulls the list from the inside pocket of her black leather jacket.

"The asshole who beat me before I passed out. He's the last thing I remember before waking up in that grave. I want to know what happened. I need him to fill the gaps in my memory before he stops breathing," she states as she studies her list for the millionth time.

"It's not going anywhere."

"I know. I just want to make sure I have every detail memorized."

I dart my eyes her way once more before pulling them back towards the road.

Before we left the clubhouse with the guys earlier today we made sure to go over each location. We covered everything from entry points to potential threats within the residence, but I can't help but to feel that we're missing something. I'm not sure if it's just me being anxious and paranoid about bringing along an untrained civilian, or if there's more to it. I guess only time will tell.

Chapter Fourteen

Charlie

Jax reaches over and rests his hand on my upper thigh giving it a small squeeze. I move my hand to cover his and give it a reassuring squeeze in return.

I know he's trying to comfort me, but I'm not sure what else I need to do to prove to him I don't need the reassurance most women probably do. I'm not a damsel in distress, though I imagine that is what I looked like walking into that bar.

Over the past few days I've experienced many firsts, but one of those firsts was the acceptance I felt last night and today from Jax and his friends and family. I've come to realize I'm stronger than I even thought I was. Compared to inside the asylum, everyone on this side of the wall feels soft, weak, sheltered maybe? I'm not sure what the right feelings are for that conclusion.

Jax thinks he's a monster from nightmares. He's yet to understand that while he may be a monster, I'm a nightmare come to life. One of their own making.

"We're almost there," he says.

There is about half a mile of trees before we reach the

house with a small turnoff about halfway down. We turn right and pull into the small trail between the trees. There's a mixture of dirt and thin patches of grass spread sporadically throughout the trail.

Jax kills the headlights and pulls in far enough so that we're hidden in the trees from any traffic that may drive past and the surrounding neighbors. I do a weapons check as we get out of the SUV, running my hands over each sleeve to make sure all of my knives are still in place.

"You ready?"

"More than ready," I reply eagerly.

He reaches over and holds my hand as he leads me through the woods. This feels oddly familiar, being surrounded by trees. Even the weather tonight and the feel of fall quickly approaching in the cool night air. The only differences being that I'm not alone and instead of being angry and in shock, I'm angry and excited. The buzzing excitement filling my veins is enough to make me smile.

I didn't pay much attention on the ride over here, which I know was stupid, considering if we get split up and I need to go back to the cabin I have no clue how to get back. *Stupid, Charlie.*

As we hide in the tree line, I take in the small white house that looks like it has seen better days with white paint peeling from the sides and a front porch that looks like it will collapse should it take any weight at all. Here's hoping it's stronger than it looks.

Jax leads me toward the house, reminding me to stay behind him. I can't help the eye roll that breaks free. In my defense, that was a hard one to hold in.

Jax leans against the bedroom wall with his arms crossed, brows pulled down in concern as he watches me hold a knife to the man's throat.

Once we were inside the house, Jax helped me strip him down and tie each wrist and ankle to the bed.

His eyes look like they might fall out of his head if he were to open them any further. I'm not sure why he seems so shaken by my being here, aside from the fact that I'm outside my prison instead of inside where he could use and abuse my body as he pleased.

Surely he already knew I wasn't there.

"What do you want?" he spits out.

"Answer my questions," I say with a smile as I press my blade a little further into his throat.

"The last thing I remember is *you*, Jarod."

He shakes his head back and forth, forgetting about the blade for a moment until it nicks him a small bit. Seeing the blood pebble on his throat gives me a small thrill and I look forward to seeing more spill from this disgusting sack of flesh.

"You know what you did. The last thing I remember is your face. What happened after you *raped* me, again, you sick fuck?" I scream in his face as I lean over him and try to block out the smell of his pungent breath.

I wait a moment and then flick my wrist causing yet another nick in his skin as I take him by surprise.

"I thought you were dead!" he cries out.

I can't help the surge of anger that bubbles from within.

Instead of a feeling of buzzing excitement it feels more like gravel churning in my stomach.

"You thought I was dead?"

He nods his head yes.

"So you fucking *buried* me?" I scream again as I bring the knife up and stab in through the palm of his hand that's tied to the post of the bed, leaving it there. I then pull out another blade from its place on my body.

"Buried me *alive*?" I yell again in disbelief as I stab the knife through his other palm, feeling the blade cut through the small bones in his hand, leaving both palms impaled.

Once again, I reach up and grab a third knife from the belt that is strapped to my body.

"Shut him up," Jax says, but I can't just yet. I have more questions.

"Dr. Whitmore. My father. Why?" I plead for an answer to a question I don't even know I'm asking, and it makes me sick that I've let my voice take on a tone that sounds weak, like they hoped I would be, instead of the survivor I know I am.

"I don't know what you're talking about!" he says as he cries out in pain like the little bitch he appears to be.

"You're nothing but a weak little bitch. Aren't you? You couldn't get anyone else to let you inside them, so you took what wasn't yours."

His eyes get a little life back into them as they dance with mirth once more. A familiar look to them. One I've seen him give before.

"I seem to remember you didn't always have a problem with letting us inside that pussy, now, did you Char?" he spits out.

I see Jax move forward out of the corner of my eye, and I'll be damned if he takes this from me.

I grab the fourth knife from my belt and back up, stabbing through his limp dick with one knife and lift it, making his flesh stand in an upward position. I take my other hand and swiftly jerk that knife in a slashing motion. I look down to see his little nub of flesh hanging from the other blade while his body continues to try to pump blood to the missing appendage.

I breathe a sigh of relief knowing that it will never be able to take from me again.

Jarod continues to scream in pain. I decide then and there that he's just as dead as he thought I was when he buried me and do us both a favor, slashing my blade across his throat to make that a reality.

Jax moves toward me again, this time coming to stand beside me. With a smile on his face he holds up his gun and puts a bullet through Jarod's forehead.

"Seriously?" I pout.

"Sorry, little terror. He was taking too long, and we need to go."

I move away from the bed and lift my hands in front of my face to mimic holding a camera in front of my eyes and move my finger down and make a clicking sound with my tongue. A mental snapshot to help me remember this night forever.

Jax removes my knives and rinses them off in the sink before we leave the house.

"Go stand at the tree line," he instructs me.

I give him a questioning look but do as he says.

Once I get to the tree line I turn around and see he's moved further away from the house and is now on the phone as he walks toward me.

Once he reaches me, he ends the call and takes my hand. I give one more glance over my shoulder at the house that held so few answers for me and can only hope that the next name on my list will be able to give me what I need.

WE ARRIVE BACK AT THE SAFE HOUSE AND JAX GRABS US both a change of clothes, meeting me in the bathroom. I've already turned the shower on, and the bathroom has filled with steam, clouding up the mirror above the sink.

I remove my clothes that are still covered in blood, and he bags them up as I step into the shower. Standing under the hot spray, I close my eyes and enjoy the feeling of my muscles beginning to relax for the first time in a while.

Arms wrap around me from behind, and I know Jax has joined me. I feel his muscular body wrap around mine from behind, his swollen member pressing against my ass. I can't help the desperate whimper that escapes my mouth.

He lowers his head to my shoulders and kisses along the side of my neck, licking and nibbling between each kiss. I lift my hands to my chest and squeeze my nipples, tweaking them between my fingers and pulling as I feel him release a satisfied groan against my skin as he watches over my shoulder.

"Is that what you like, baby? Pain with your pleasure?" he murmurs into my neck and then sinks his teeth into my shoulder, breaking the skin just enough to draw a few drops of blood.

"Yes!" I pant as I drop one hand and reach behind me to wrap my hand around his cock as it's pressed against me.

Jax starts to move his hand south on my body, but I want to make sure he receives just as much pleasure from my mouth as I did from his.

I slowly turn around and kiss my way down his chest and his stomach as I lower onto my knees. I take in the size of his swollen cock only looking up into his eyes once I lick the pre-cum from his heavy tip.

"Fuck, Charlie," Jax hisses through his teeth as he looks back at me just as determined as I am looking at him.

I lick up and down each side of his length and then spit on his cock to get it nice and wet for me to stroke. I take his balls into my mouth entirely and suck while pulling down and out while stroking his cock back and forth at the same time. I can't help the whimper I release as I feel the slickness grow between my legs.

"I want inside you," he says while groaning.

"Fuck me please?" I whisper as I pull my mouth from his balls.

He then pulls away and bends down to help me up. Or at least that's what I think he's doing, until my feet come off of the ground. I then wrap my legs around his waist.

I notice he left the shower running as he walks us out of the bathroom, bodies still wet and dripping both from the shower and from desire.

"How do you want it baby?" he asks softly.

"Hard. Fuck me like you hate me."

"Careful, little terror, there's a thin line between love and hate. It may be hard to tell which one I'm chasing."

I laugh as he lowers my feet to the floor, then crawl onto the bed on my hands and knees, turning around with my ass in the air on all fours. I glance over my shoulder and smirk at his hungry eyes, breaking the last of his restraint.

He climbs onto the bed and his thick, heavy cock seeks entrance to my core. I push back against his length, impaling my pussy with one hard thrust.

Chapter Fifteen

Jax

Heaven. I thought for sure I would end up in hell, but here I am, balls deep in heaven herself.

I tighten my grip on her hips with both hands.

"Goddamn, baby. Rough is what you want, then that's what you'll get," I tell her.

I rut my cock into her hard and as fast, scooting us both across the bed as she makes the most delicious sounds.

I reach down and grab her long wet purple hair, wrap it around my wrist and tug sharply, jolting her head back. I draw my other hand back and smack her ass, leaving an instant blush to her pale, perfectly rounded cheek.

"You love this dick?"

"Yes!" she replies.

"Whose dick is it, baby?"

"Mine."

"I can't hear you."

"My dick! Mine!" she cries out as I smack her ass twice more.

"That's right, little terror, and whose pussy is this?"

I reach beneath us and smack her swollen pearl, sending her over the edge into madness.

"Yours! Your pussy!" she screams as she coats my cock with her sweet cream.

After a few more thrusts I reach down and pinch her clit mid climax, causing her to erupt, squirting her juices all over my shaft and balls as I pump thick ropes of my cum deep inside her tight hot cunt.

Charlie continues to shake as both of us come down from the high of not only our heated encounter, but also crossing a name off the list earlier in the night.

She collapses onto the bed, and I fall in beside her. She's wearing a lazy grin as she continues to breathe heavily. I can see she's deep in thought.

"What are you thinking?" I ask.

She turns to face me, raises her head, and presses her lips to mine. Once, twice, and then lowers her head back to the pillow. I reach up and stroke her hair, moving it out of her face.

"I'm thinking your water bill is going to be a little high this month."

"Worth it," I say, wearing a cocky grin and not an ounce of regret to be found.

A FEW DAYS HAVE PASSED SINCE CHARLIE MADE HER first kill. We've stayed at the cabin since that night.

I've touched base with Ashlyn to make sure everything is okay there and that she's not having any problems with customers at the bar. She's a tough one, but I generally come around pretty often to look after her and most people know she's not one to be messed with.

I've also been in contact with Liam, Wren, and Kai at the clubhouse. They're helping us with a few things. I called them after we left the body in the house the other night and they sent out a cleaner.

I usually clean up after myself. I would much rather do my own cleaning than leave my freedom in the hands of a stranger, but if they trust him, I do, too.

"Are you sure there isn't another way in?" Charlie mumbles.

"I'm sure."

The next step of her "bloody plan" is an important one. One that could change everything, and it seems they have an elaborate security system to match their rank of importance. The guys running backend are on location for this one, helping us disable the security for the gate and motion sensors along with any that might be on the house itself.

Just like before, Charlie follows me over the gate. We decided though the perimeter alarms may be disabled we don't want to take a chance opening the gate, so we climbed it instead. It's not my first choice, but rather safe than sorry.

We make our way to the back of the estate. The large mansion sits on about twenty acres of land. The house is a luxury craftsman style home with a mix of brown brick and wooden accents. It has a cottage feel, but about ten times bigger in square footage.

The guys are on coms and give us the go ahead to enter. We studied the floor plan before we left the cabin.

"You sure you want to do this?" I whisper.

"I'm sure. It's a piece of my story that needs to be put in its place."

Shit.

The last time she told me anything about *her story* I got lost in my head and my past with my own story.

She squeezes my hand in reassurance and we head through the back entryway, make our way through several rooms before we reach the one we're hoping to find.

I'm sure at one point this house was full of family and love, one can only hope, but right now its barren and depressing as hell.

I raise my gun as we enter the room. What we find is both heartbreaking and satisfying. Without knowing if her mother's father, Charlie's grandfather, had anything to do with any of this we're left with nothing. On one hand if he did, it would be appealing to see him hooked to machines and receiving hospice care. On the other hand, if he was innocent in all of this, this is a piece of Charlie's family that she'll never know.

It's fucked up how unbalanced life is sometimes. I don't say unfair because who's to say what fair even is, but you can't tell me that a girl who survived everything she has only to be left with no real family or answers is a balance. Not saying I believe in Karma because if that's real I'm pretty fucked myself. I guess we'll just have to keep searching for answers.

I take a look at Charlie, and she stands there motionless with her face free of any expression at all. I don't think she knows what to think or feel.

I give her a few minutes to decide on his fate.

"Let's go," she says in a whisper.

I give her one more look and she nods her head to let me know she's sparing him. I can understand why. I wouldn't wish the guilt on her if we later found out that he's innocent. He's near the end of his life anyway. No need to rush it along when the end is inevitable either way.

We make our way back downstairs only for Charlie to be suddenly jerked and she falls to the floor. I turn in time to see a dead man walking, and he's charging toward her.

I lift my gun and shoot him in the same place she was shot, her shoulder. I quickly check on Charlie and she's fine. So I shoot him in both knees to make sure he can't go anywhere and disarm him as quickly as possible.

Charlie's getting back up by the time I get back to her.

"Motherfucker!" she yells at the man. The man who we find out is her uncle. Her mother's brother. He was next so this is a two for one and with the events playing out in front of us he won't be breathing when we leave here. If she doesn't end him, I will.

She goes right to the nearest bathroom and finds a couple towels to help put pressure on her wound. We tie one around her arm and shoulder to apply pressure and use the other to make a sling.

Once she's taken care of I drag this asshole down to the wine cellar and Charlie follows behind us with nothing but rage blanketing her face.

Chapter Sixteen

Charlie

Not much shocks me in this world. I'm not really an optimist or a pessimist. I don't really do the glass half empty or half full. I choose option C. Break the fucking glass and empty that bitch yourself. Fragile things will shatter. That's just the way it is. So make sure you're not one of those breakable things.

I've spent my entire life with filth who wanted nothing more than to break me. There were times when I thought they did. I even let them for a while. But something inside me told me to never let them win. So I didn't and here I am.

My own fucking uncle just shot me. I can't help but wonder if he knows who I am. I'm sure he does. I look just like my mother. If only I could reach out to her, but I need to take care of these things first. Then I can get her out of that place.

I'm down an arm so Jax gets *Uncle* Dave tied to a chair. I'm already over it so I cut right to the chase.

"What the hell are you doing?" I ask, and I receive his obnoxious laughter in return.

"I'm protecting my investment," he replies.

"What exactly did you invest in?"

He forces out another fake laugh. He's trying to play it off as if he's not sitting there with two blown out kneecaps and a bullet hole in his shoulder that mirrors mine.

"Did you enjoy your time in Oak Grove Asylum?" he asks.

This...nope. I'm not letting him see me yell and rant like a mad woman. Instead, I walk over to one of the wine racks and grab a bottle, busting it on the edge of the shelf. No telling how much this bottle of wine costs, but I'm sure it's not cheap.

I take long strides back to his chair and hold the neck of the bottle as I push it up to his throat.

"I want answers, and something tells me you have them. Talk," I demand.

He smiles.

I lift the bottle up and drag the jagged edge down the side of his face, cutting deep crooked lines into his skin that are sure to scar.

He screams in pain.

"Talk."

Again, he laughs, but only seconds go by before he starts rambling information off. His pride won out after all. He just has to pour salt in the wound. He can't pass up a chance to take credit for the pain he's caused. Of course he couldn't resist. He may be in with the elite, but what do you know? Apparently, class can't be bought after all.

"Your mother wasn't crazy. I mean yeah. She had her issues. Schizophrenia and a mood imbalance. Too bad she didn't notice me changing out her meds." He laughs, but it sounds more like wheezing with the pain he's starting to feel as some of the adrenaline from being shot wears off.

Jax decides to take a seat now that Dave is talking and

turns the chair around in the corner straddling it with the gun still in Jax's hand.

"She was always the favorite. I overheard Dad talking about cutting me out of the will because some stupid bitch claimed I raped her. Lying ass whore. So I made sure Charlotte got sent away for good," he says with a smile.

"But then the good old doctor couldn't keep it in his fucking pants now could he?"

My head snaps back to him where I had started to wander in my thoughts.

With a smile he goes on to tell us how my mother found a way to hide the pregnancy until it was too late, and she was close to giving birth. She had refused to talk and continued to act the same way she did when she was sedated so they didn't see a need for the meds. Some baggy sweatshirts and eventually she was going into labor. My father took her down to a lab where he delivered me. He locked her away to take care of me and once I was starting to walk and talk they moved her back to the patient rooms and me along with her.

Other employees knew not to ask questions.

Apparently she had tried to escape with me several times when they weren't giving her the drugs, but she never made it past the gate. The same sad story that I had when I made my attempts to escape years later. I never made it past the gate, until I was carried out as an alleged corpse.

"So let me get this straight. You were jealous of my mom and wanted even more money than what you already had? That's why you set my mother up for a life of misery, and left us both to rot even after you found out about her having a daughter?" I ask incredulously.

"That's what I said." He begins to mumble as he starts looking more drowsy by the minute.

Jax stands up pulling a pack out of his pocket and cracking it under Dave's nose causing him to jump and sit up straighter, looking more alert than before.

"You're a fucking gutter whore. Same as your mother. But she's gone so no need to worry about her now," he says with a chuckle.

I snap my eyes to Jax, and he keeps his expression unreadable. I can tell by that alone he knew she was dead. I want to rant and rave. I want to be furious with him, but I can't.

I never said anything about saving her. I guess I just assumed that was a given. I don't think he knows I didn't know she was dead already.

Inside my heart feels like it's breaking. I may have trouble with my emotions sometimes, but this one is clearly loss. I do what I do best and lock it away. He can never know I didn't already have that missing piece of the story. He may call himself the monster or the villain, but regardless, he has a big heart. Even if he can be a dick at times.

I won't put that burden on him. He's done too much for me already. I'll carry this one alone.

Jax taught me the basics of shooting a gun over the past few days and even had me outside shooting at targets. So we decided I would pack one as a backup.

I've gotten everything I needed out of this man. And quite frankly, I'm over it.

I reach into the holster next to where I wear my knives, draw the gun, and move closer since I'm not a very good shot yet, and pull the trigger putting two bullets in his head the same way I saw Jax do last time we killed a man.

Jax looks at me as if he's surprised. I can see why. I surprised myself too.

"I'll clean up. I want to make sure it's done right since

your DNA is all over the place upstairs from your blood. Liam is handling the home health nurse situation, getting one sent out, but not until we leave."

I nod in understanding and sit down in the chair he was sitting in just moments ago. My adrenaline is crashing fast, and the pain isn't helping anything tonight, but I try to help how I can.

A couple hours later, we're back over the fence and on our way back to the cabin after the nurse arrives, who hasn't the slightest clue as to what just took place in that house.

Chapter Seventeen

Jax

Charlie has spent the last two weeks recovering from the gunshot wound her uncle inflicted. During that time we've made it back to town a couple times to check on Ashlyn and even stop into the diner to check on Mrs. Sonny and grab some chili cheese-burgers and crinkle cut fries to take back to the cabin with us. Charlie loves them even more than I do. I think it's because she has had no choice but to appreciate the finer things in life like food and water. To her they were simply a luxury before she was on the outside, but now that she's here, she can have as much as she wants.

The joy she gets from things we take for granted warms a place in my cold dead heart, and I could swear I even feel it beat once or twice.

"YOU WANT PROOF? HERE'S YOUR PROOF," CHARLIE says as she holds the results in front of her face.

"A product of rape only to be locked away in a prison by my own sperm donor and left for whatever wolves came around to scrounge for fresh meat," she adds.

"I hope you've enjoyed your fancy Ivy League bullshit and country club days because my disgusting *uncle* was the one funding your frivolous lifestyle. It only took me being raped whenever they pleased for you to live a life of luxury. You're welcome."

Charlie lays it all out for them with a smirk on her face. I'm proud of her. Not backing down or feeling less than. She's earned the right to be treated with respect, not that she needed to.

"Please. Just let us go. I had no idea about any of this," his wife begs as she cries. Her daughter crying just as much if not harder.

We discovered ahead of time they're telling the truth. We know they had no idea any of this was going on all these years. The guys even found evidence of domestic violence against his wife. There was nothing to find about him with their daughter, but that doesn't mean anything. You never know with a man like that.

After Charlie made several threats she let them pack some necessities and sent them on their way, with a promise they'd never return. Sister or not, she wanted nothing to do with them.

She saved the best for last. It took some time but once Dr. Whitmore returned home we set him up in a nice little makeshift lab and strapped him to an exam table.

"Now don't worry. You won't feel a thing," Charlie said with a sugary sweet smile as she proceeded to shock her father with the same machine he had used on her.

After everything she's learned over the past several weeks, we concluded that she was missing some chunks of time, most likely retrograde amnesia thanks to her father playing with the machine she's currently using on his mind.

She spent quite a lot of time playing with the machine until we got worried he may pass out and not wake up from the seizures it seemed to induce.

I watched as she pulled out the equipment we had brought with us and cracked into his chest while he was still conscious.

I loved seeing her work. I always got the most turned on when she was in her element and enjoying herself, whether she was drowning in someone else's blood or drinking a glass of water. If she enjoyed it, I did too.

Love and hate. Not sure which I was chasing, my ass.

Chapter Eighteen

Charlie

I'm not sure if he passed out from blood loss, the electroshock therapy, or the pain itself, but he eventually did. Unfortunately, I'm pretty sure that's when he died. Shortly after I cut open his chest. I was at least hoping to hold his beating heart in the palm of my hand.

Maybe in the next life.

"Look at that, Dad. You broke before me," I said to his lifeless body with a satisfied grin.

I turn around to look at Jax and see him trying to adjust himself. I don't think he understands there's no hiding it and that's one of the many things I...yeah.

"You ready?" he asks.

"Ready," I reply.

After everything we've been through, I'm exhausted and ready for this to just be over.

Part of me wanted to cage my father for years like he did me, but another part thought I shouldn't waste any more time on someone so vile. That part won.

We leave the house and get to the gate when Jax stops me.

"What's wrong?" I ask as I pull my brows down in concern.

"I have a surprise for you," he says with that cocky grin of his in place.

"And what might that be?"

He hands me a remote and all I can do is stare at it in confusion. He places his arms on my shoulders and turns me around, pointing at the house and then eyeing the remote with the big shiny button.

"Oh, hell yeah!" I say with excitement as I move my finger faster than I even knew possible and push that button, causing the house of my many horrors to explode into a beautiful, fiery ball of flames.

We stay until the fire department comes and then drift away into the night, leaving behind the last of the shattered pieces of my old life.

3 Months Later

I lay on my stomach on the dead grass and run my fingers along the bouquet propped up against the headstone. There's something about flowers on a grave that gives me peace of mind, or maybe even hope. Someone cared enough to bring them to the grave and visit whoever lies beneath the dirt.

I was wearing a coat and everything else that goes along with winter gear when I arrived, though I can't help but pull it all off as I extend my arms and lay my head down, pressing my cheek to the cold, frozen ground.

"Here lies Charlie," I murmur as I read the words on my headstone and try harder to press a hug to the ground. I really wish I could give my old self a hug and tell her how proud I am of her.

When she climbed out of this shallow grave, she had no idea what kind of world was waiting for her or the plans she would set in motion wreaking havoc on all who wronged her with a man who chose to stay by her side no matter what came for her.

A few weeks ago, my grandfather's power of attorney contacted me to inform me that his estate was now mine because of his passing. I have a sneaking suspicion Jax and the guys worked this out to land in my favor.

I have no idea what to do with millions of dollars, so the first thing I bought was a headstone to memorialize the grave I climbed out of, letting it represent rebirth.

I look up and see Jax sitting on the ground with his back pressed against the headstone. This has become our place lately. He finds meaning in it, the same as me.

He holds his hand out, and I sit up on my knees and crawl to him. He lifts me up and I straddle his lap, running my fingernails through his hair, scratching down his scalp. He lets out a groan as I close the distance, pressing my lips to his.

I look up into his eyes and set the words free.

"I love you, Jaxton Jameson Jagger," I say for the first time with a playful smile. It's taken me a while, but I know the feeling now and there's no denying it.

The lust blazing in his eyes is enough to have me reaching down and unbuttoning his jeans.

"I love you, too, little terror," he says with more feeling than I could have imagined.

He helps me shift his pants down as I practically climb

out of mine, ignoring the cold winter air. I straddle him once more and slowly sink on to his stiff length. I'm already slick from craving him all afternoon as he teased me, edging me to the point of madness and then coming to a full stop.

I swivel my hips as I ride his cock faster, rocking hard enough to gain friction on my bundle of nerves.

"That's it. Ride that cock, baby," he demands.

"I love the way your cock fills me up." I whimper as I run my hands through his hair, slamming my pussy down on his shaft and then grinding once again.

"You going to let me suck my cum out of you and clean that pretty pussy after I finish fucking it so good?" he grinds out through clenched teeth, while trying to stay in control.

"Yes! I want to taste your cum on your tongue so bad."

He grabs my neck with one hand, squeezing hard enough to make me struggle for air, causing my core to tighten around him as the heat in my lower belly spreads south.

I feel his shaft pulsate as my vision gets spotty, and he fucks me harder from the below, meeting me thrust for thrust.

I can't help but cry out as my core floods his cock, dripping down his balls.

A few thrusts later, and Jax lets out a demanding growl as he shoots his cum deep within my walls.

He lifts me off of him, sets my bare ass on the cold headstone, spreads my legs and dips his tongue between my folds, fucking and sucking my cunt until every drop of him is resting on his tongue. He stands up and leans over me, tilting my head back.

"Open," he commands while rubbing my lips with his thumb.

I do as he says and am rewarded as he spits his cum into my mouth.

He leans down, kissing me again, massaging his tongue against mine as I swallow a mixture of my cream and his seed down my throat together.

I can't help but sigh in contentment as we both stand and get dressed once again.

"Maybe one of the guys can join us next time?" I ask jokingly, only because I love how possessive he can be.

He comes to an abrupt stop and furrows his brows.

"You're a wicked woman. You know that?" he says as he scoops me up and throws me over his shoulder in a fireman's hold, smacking me on the ass.

"Who's the wicked one now?" I ask with a laugh.

THE END

A Note From The Author

Thank you so much for taking the time to read about Charlie and Jax! I really hope you enjoyed their story!

My goal was to give you a full length novel, but we aren't quite there yet. I do plan to possibly extend this novella into a novel at a later date. Even as I type these words I can hear Charlie and Jax screaming in my head.

If you'd like to hear more of their story please feel free to reach out and let me know!

Acknowledgments

To my husband. Even though I said I might one day be on an episode of Snapped, you continue to encourage me. Thank you for that. Lol It's because of you that I write again and have the courage to hit publish each time. I love you.

To my son, who better not have his eyes anywhere near these pages. It makes my heart happy every time you cheer me on, and you cheer me on every single day no matter what I'm doing. Lol Love you, bub.

RJ Creatives. Thank you for the awesome cover and bringing my vision to life.

Amy. Unfortunately, I didn't have the Acknowledgments written for you to edit in time so please excuse all of the errors. I'm thankful that you didn't have to tell me the difference in spelling come and cum this time! I bet you are, too.

Unalive Promotions for the book tours and formatting. You're pretty fucking cool. I wonder why? *wink*

To my Crimson Queens and all the readers, bookstagrammers, booktokers, bloggers. Thank you so much for just being you. Your encouragement and support is everything to me. Thank you for sharing, reading, reviewing, yelling, and screaming about my books to anyone who will listen. I love you all.

About the Author

Tristina Brockway is living the good life.

She lives in her pajamas and she's seriously addicted to the nectar of life– maybe better known as caramel Macchiatos. While she's a self proclaimed bitch, she's not the only one in the household. They also have a rescue dog named Bella, as well as two new KitKats, Oreo and Trix. Tristina is all about rescuing fur babies, and most days she prefers them to people.

Tristina counts sarcasm as her second language, and her humor is so dark she probably shouldn't be telling Knock Knock jokes in public.

Reading and writing are her main hobbies and she loves strong female leads, reverse harem, dark romance, paranormal and taboo stories. She ugly cries with just about any book she reads. She's a cheat reader who needs to read the last page before she dives in, just so she can mentally prepare herself and check her expectations.

www.tristinabrockway.com

Join the Crimson Queen's Readers Group on Facebook!

facebook.com/authortristinabrockway

instagram.com/authortristinabrockway

amazon.com/stores/Tristina-
Brockway/author/B08HRGGVJD

bookbub.com/authors/tristina-brockway

goodreads.com/authortristinabrockway

pinterest.com/tristinab

tiktok.com/@authortristinabrockway

Also by Tristina Brockway

CRIMSON QUEENS DUET

Her Crimson Reign Book #1

Secrets Inside Me Book #2

NOVELLAS

When The Wicked Play

Made in the USA
Las Vegas, NV
13 July 2023